I Love You More Than...

Written By Bree Goldstein

Illustrated by Elaine Hasford

For Shale
Love, Mom

To my first niece & nephew, thank you for being my inspiration while I waited to meet you.

Isaac, I've loved you for more than your whole life because I've loved your mom for all of mine.

Aunt-E

I love you
more
than
all the
stars
in the
sky!

I love you
more
than
the
peaches
in a
pie!

I love you more
than
craters on the moon!

I love you
more
than
a
bright
red
balloon!

I love you more than the sprinkles on ice cream!

I love you more
than tricks
on a balance beam!

I love you more
than all the
herbs in tea!

I love you
more
than
the
fish
in the
sea!

I love you
more
than
all the
apples
in
juice!

I love you
more
than
the
feathers
on a
goose!

I love you
more
than
the
petals
on a
flower!

I love you
more
than
all the
drops
in a
shower!

I love you
more
than
all the
points
in a
tennis
match!

I love you more
than all the seeds
in a pumpkin patch!

I love you more
than all the
cars on the road!

I love you
more
than
all the
computer
code!

I love you
more
than
the
beads
on a
necklace!

I love you more
than the
cacti in Texas!

I love you more
than the
words in this book!

I love you more
than
capturing a rook!

I love you
more
than
flames
from
a
campfire!

I love you more
than clothes
fresh from the dryer!

I love you
more
than
the
colors
in the
rainbow!

I love you more
than all the whistles
that trains blow!

I love you more than
strawberries in smoothies!

I love you more
than
popcorn at the movies!

I love you
more
than
the
toys
in a
chest!

I love you
more
than
answers
on a
test!

I love you more
than all the
bricks in a tower!

I love you
more
than
all the
royals
in
power!

I love you
more
than
a
panda
loves
bamboo!

I love you
most
because you're you!

The End

Made in the USA
Lexington, KY
07 February 2017